**W9-CAG-299**

OFFICIALLY NOTED

MONROEVILLE PUBLIC LIBRARY
4000 GATEWAY CAMPUS BLVD
MONROEVILLE, PA 15146

# The Best Gift

by Anne Marie Ryan

Illustrated by Florencia Denis

Reading Consultant: Susan Nations, M.Ed.

NEW
FOREST
PRESS

Publisher: Tim Cook

Editor: Valerie J. Weber

Designer: Steve West

ISBN: 978 1 84898 507 0

Library of Congress Control Number: 2011924938

U.S. publication © 2011 New Forest Press
Published in arrangement with Black Rabbit Books

PO Box 784, Mankato, MN 56002
www.newforestpress.com

Printed in the USA

15 14 13 12 11 1 2 3 4 5

All rights reserved. No part of this publication may be reproduced,
copied, stored in a retrieval system, or transmitted in any form or by any
means electronic, mechanical, photocopying, recording, or otherwise
without prior written permission of the copyright owner.

# How to Use This Book

*The Best Gift* is perfect for children who are just starting to learn to read. This book focuses on the *cvcc* (consonant-vowel-consonant-consonant) words.

## The Sounds in This Book

Before reading the story, turn to page 24. The grid explains how to pronounce all of the sounds in the story.

## Difficult Words

Words in bold in the text do not sound exactly like they look. Children will need help with the difficult part of the word, which is underlined below. The difficult part of the word may not fit the usual rules about what the letter sounds like or the reader may not have learned it yet.

| Difficult words in this book: | | | |
|---|---|---|---|
| <u>the</u> | h<u>er</u> | <u>I</u> | h<u>a</u>ve |
| s<u>ai</u>d | m<u>y</u> | h<u>e</u> | d<u>oes</u> |

To help struggling readers, make flashcards of the difficult words. Ask the reader to find the difficult part within the word, identify the sound, and say the whole word.

Bess has made a test.

**The** best gift in **the** land
will win **her** hand.

"**I** must win," **said** Jack.

OFFICIALLY NOTED

But Jack **does** not **have** much,
just his dog Sam.

Zack got Bess a lamp.

"It is dull!" **said** Bess.

Russ got Bess a silk quilt.

"It is dull!" **said** Bess.

Max got Bess a red belt.

"It is dull!" **said** Bess.

Jack felt sad.
**He** had no gift for Bess.

But Sam can help.

Sam ran off fast.

Jump! Sam sat on Bess.

Bess got a lick. Sam got a pat.

"A pet is **the** best gift yet!"
**said** Bess.

"Jack wins **my** hand."

# More about Phonics

Spoken English uses more than 40 speech sounds. Each sound is called a *phoneme*. Some phonemes relate to a single letter (d-o-g) and others to combinations of letters (sh-ar-p). When a phoneme is written down, it is called a *grapheme*. Teaching these sounds, matching them to their written form, and sounding out words for reading is the basis of phonics.

Early phonics instruction gives children the tools to sound out, blend, and say the words without having to rely on memory or guesswork. This instruction gives children the confidence and ability to read unfamiliar words, helping them progress toward independent reading.

# About the Consultant

Susan Nations (M.Ed.) is a reading consultant, author, and literacy coach. She is National Board Certified in the area of Literacy and has a Reading Endorsement. Nations has spent more than 25 years working in early education. Currently, she is an intervention teacher and works with students and teachers to implement and improve literacy instruction and acquisition.

# A Pronunciation Guide

All of the sounds in this grid are in the story.

| | | | |
|---|---|---|---|
| s <br> as in *sat* | a <br> as in *ant* | t <br> as in *tin* | p <br> as in *pig* |
| i <br> as *ink* | n <br> as in *net* | c <br> as in *cat* | e <br> as in *egg* |
| h <br> as in *hen* | r <br> as in *rat* | m <br> as in *mug* | d <br> as in *dog* |
| g <br> as in *get* | o <br> as in *ox* | u <br> as in *up* | l <br> as in *log* |
| f <br> as in *fan* | b <br> as in *bag* | j <br> as in *jug* | w <br> as in *wet* |
| z <br> as in *zip* | y <br> as in *yet* | k <br> as in *kit* | qu <br> as in *quiz* |
| x <br> as in *box* | ff <br> as in *off* | ll <br> as in *fill* | ss <br> as in *hiss* |
| ck <br> as in *duck* | ch <br> as in *chip* | | |

Be careful not to add an *uh* sound to s, t, p, c, h, r, m, d, g, l, f, and b. For example, say "*fff*," not "*fuh*," and "*sss*," not "*suh*."